KT-394-414

Contents

THE CURSE
OF THE SKULL

JUNE CREBBIN

Illustrations by

DEREK BRAZELL

WALKER BOOKS
AND SUBSIDIARIES

LONDON · BOSTON · SYDNEY

For Philip,
who collected skulls

First published 1997 by Walker Books Ltd
87 Vauxhall Walk, London SE11 5HJ

This edition published 1998

2 4 6 8 10 9 7 5 3

Text © 1997 June Crebbin
Illustrations © 1997 Derek Brazell

The right of June Crebbin to be identified as author
of this work has been asserted by her in accordance with the
Copyright, Designs and Patents Act 1988.

This book has been typeset in Plantin.

Printed and bound in Great Britain
by The Guernsey Press Co. Ltd

British Library Cataloguing in Publication Data
A catalogue record for this book is
available from the British Library.

ISBN 0-7445-6012-8

J109,387 £3.99

Chapter 1

Tom's still my best friend. Even after what happened. Mum's not happy about it, but then she never has been. She says I'm easily led. Led into trouble, she means, with Tom doing the leading. But I like Tom. And he'd never done anything wrong, not really wrong, until what happened with the skull.

Tom's mad, you see. Mad about bones.

He lives across the street from me and in his garage he keeps this huge collection of skulls and skeletons. He's got the jawbone of a cow, lots of bird skulls, even a cat's skull – and hundreds of mice skeletons. You wouldn't believe how many bottles people leave in lay-bys and then, when mice creep into them for shelter, or for what's left at the bottom, they can't get out. I think it's sad. But Tom and his Dad just collect the bottles, bring them home, rinse them out and clean up the bones.

One weekend, Tom found the skull of a sheep. He fetched me across to see it. It was still dirty then, with bits of skin and flesh sticking to it but I knew it would soon be cleaned and labelled.

Tom always takes his latest find to school to show Mrs Buckley and she gets him to tell the class about it and point out various details. I knew she'd be getting the sheep's skull on her desk pretty soon.

But I was wrong.

Something happened that knocked the sheep's skull right out of Tom's head.

One Saturday Tom was round at our house, giving his mother a break. She needed lots of rest because of the new baby on the way. He wanted to play football in our garden but Mum was going to the church to do the flowers and she said we had to go with her. Tom didn't want to go. He'd never been in a church.

"It's not so bad," I told him.

I like our church. It's spooky but sort of peaceful as well.

"There's some good statues," I said.

My favourite statue is the one of the soldier

falling from his horse in battle. Mum says they buried his body underneath the statue. I thought Tom might be interested in that. But, as it turned out, he found something else far more interesting.

When we got to the church, which is just across the lane from the bottom of our garden, the door was open. We went inside and I was wrong about it being peaceful. Hammering and banging echoed round the walls.

"They're putting in the new boiler," said Mum.

We went to see. Behind the seats was a huge hole. In it, a couple of workmen were hammering away at some pipes.

"Hello," said Mum as soon as the hammering ceased for a moment. "Working overtime?"

One of the men climbed up out of the hole. "Could say that," he said. "Can't do much more though. Not until the new parts arrive." He and Mum moved away, chatting together.

I thought I'd take Tom on a tour of the statues then. But he was staring at the opposite side of the hole. The floor was covered with bones, but Tom was staring at one in particular.

"Wow!" he said. "Jack! *Look!*"

It was a human skull.

Chapter 2

"Can I have that?" said Tom.

"What?" said the workman who was still in the hole.

"That," said Tom. "That skull."

The workman laughed. "What would you be doing with a skull?" he said.

"I collect them," said Tom. "I've got all sorts of animal skulls but I haven't got a human skull."

"And you're not having this one," said the workman. "More than my job's worth. We've got to put all these bones back where we found them." He turned away.

"Can't I just hold it?" said Tom. "I only want to look."

The workman seemed doubtful. Then he reached up above him and handed it over.

Tom held the skull in his hands. I wouldn't have touched it. I thought of all the years it had lain in the ground. I thought of the person it had once been.

"Perfect," breathed Tom. "Look at the eye sockets, Jack. They're huge."

The skull seemed to grin up at us.

"Ugh," I said. "Put it back, quick."

But Tom tried again. "Are you sure I can't have it?" he said. "Who would know?"

"If you took that skull," said the workman, "a curse would fall on you. Dreadful things would happen." He winked at me as if to say, "Only joking!", but I shuddered all the same.

He reached up and took the skull out of Tom's hands.

I showed Tom the statues then, but he wasn't really interested. Suddenly he said, "Let's help your mum."

I was surprised. So was Mum.

Tom picked up the sheet with the dead flowers in. "Where do these go?" he asked.

"In the dustbin round the back," said Mum. "Thank you, Tom. That's very kind."

"I'll help, too," I said. But when we got to the door, Tom snatched the sheet away from me. "I can do it," he hissed. "You do something else."

I couldn't think why he was suddenly being

so nasty. But I got the message. I went to fetch the water from the tap by the gate.

I saw Tom tipping the bits into the dustbin and going back into the church, but I wasn't rushing to join him again. I took a long time over filling the jug.

When we'd done the flowers, Mum took us to the park. Tom had brought his sports bag with him but I noticed his football wasn't inside it. He was carrying the football under his arm. I never thought anything else might be in the bag. If I'd guessed ... but even then I suppose it was too late.

We had a good kick-around at the park. Tom was as nice as pie. He even took a turn at being the goalie and letting me shoot at him. And when he went home, he said, "Come and see my latest find."

"I've seen it," I said. I mean, there's a limit to how many times you want to see the skull of a sheep.

"No, you haven't," said Tom. "Not *properly*!"

He was hopping about with excitement. Then he went serious. *"Come on,"* he said.

So I went.

Tom took me straight into his garage. I waited for him to lift the sheep's skull down from the shelf and go on about it.

But he didn't.

Instead, he unzipped his sports bag. Then I knew why he'd been carrying his football under his arm.

Inside the sports bag was the skull – the human skull, the one I thought had been left behind in the church.

"What have you done?" I shouted.

"What does it look like?" said Tom. He lifted out the skull lovingly.

"Yes, but how...?"

"It's all right," said Tom. "No one saw me." He grinned. "Clever, wasn't I?"

I wanted to hit him.

"But you'll have to take it back," I said. "There's a curse on it."

I knew what a curse was like – rats tearing

out your insides, ghosts haunting you night after night, a terrible illness striking you down...

"You've got to take it back," I said. "Before it's too late!"

Tom fingered the skull.

"I can't," he said.

At that moment, Tom's black cat came into the garage.

"Have it your own way," I said. "But don't blame me if Sooty disappears and never comes back." I'd read a horror story where a pet rabbit disappeared and was found bubbling in a pot on top of the oven. "Don't say I didn't warn you."

Sooty wound herself round Tom's legs, purring like an engine, but when Tom leaned down to stroke her, she ran away.

"See!" I cried. "See. She knows the skull is cursed!"

Tom stood up.

"Well, I don't believe any of it," he said. "She's just a stupid old cat."

He cleared a place in the middle of the top shelf. "There," he said, positioning the skull. "My best yet."

I couldn't believe he was going to keep it.

"You're mad," I said.

"No, I'm not," said Tom. He looked at the skull proudly. I'd seen the same expression a hundred times on the faces of the mums who gathered at our school gates showing off their new babies.

But I couldn't just give up.

"What about your dad?" I said. "*He'll* go mad when he finds out. You *have* stolen it – or are you forgetting that?"

I knew what my dad would say if I stole something.

Tom swung round.

"I'll just say I found it," he said. "I don't have to say where, do I?"

I pointed to his shelves, to the labels. "You do," I said. "When and where. They all say where."

"Oh, shut up!" Tom shouted. But then he

reached up and took the skull off the shelf.

For a moment I thought, he's changed his mind, and I felt relieved. I mean, the curse could have affected me too. Of course *I* hadn't stolen it, I hadn't even touched it, but I was in the know. I felt part of it.

"You could take it back now," I suggested. "I'll go with you."

Tom looked at me as though he was dealing with a dumb-brain. "I'm not taking it back," he said. He put the skull in his sports bag. "I'm taking it to school. Wait till Mrs Buckley sees this!"

Chapter 3

Back at home, I couldn't stop thinking about what had happened. I couldn't get to sleep that night for worrying about it and when I did manage to drop off, I had a terrible dream – a soldier in full dress uniform but *with no head* kept chasing me, mounted on his magnificent black charger, across miles and miles of desert, shouting, "Give me back my head! What have you done with my head?"

I worried about the curse all Sunday and by Monday morning I was exhausted. When Tom called for me on his way to school, he had his sports bag with him. I let myself hope just for a moment it might contain his usual stuff. No chance.

"Can't wait to show everyone," he said as we set off. He tapped the bag significantly and then he tapped his nose three times. My heart sank.

"Mrs Buckley will want to know where you found it," I said. "She won't like it."

"She'll be gobsmacked." Tom grinned.

I didn't doubt that, but with the skull came the curse. My dreams had already been haunted by a headless ghost. I was worried sick we were about to see the curse in action a second time, bringing down Mrs Buckley's anger on us both.

There were two people who wanted to show things to the class that day. Tom and Milly Bateman. Milly had a group of girls round her when we went in.

"What've you got?" I said. There was a biscuit tin on her desk, with holes in it. "What've you got in there? Give us a look."

"Not likely," said Milly Bateman. "Too dangerous!" She and the other girls giggled.

Showing things in our class isn't like when we were Infants. Then, we just stood up, showed what we'd brought, said a few words and sat down again. Now we were in Year 6, we were expected to give a full-blown talk – and everyone was supposed to listen and ask intelligent questions at the end.

Mrs Buckley did the register. Then she said Tom should go first.

I could hardly bear to watch. There was a gasp as he lifted the skull out of his sports bag, and even a scream from some people. I knew every eye was on him. Except mine. I was watching Mrs Buckley.

Her mouth dropped open but by then Tom had launched into his talk.

I kept thinking Mrs Buckley would interrupt him, stop him, do something, but she didn't. At the end, though, she didn't wait for questions. She had a question of her own.

"Well, that was very interesting, Tom," she said. She sounded calm. "You're very lucky to have a human skull. Wherever did you find it?"

There was the tiniest pause. Then – "In the church," Tom said. Just like that. I mean, I'd expected him to try and make something up. I knew he'd tell the truth in the end but I'd expected him to try one or two variations to start with.

"In the church," repeated Mrs Buckley.

"In the ground," said Tom helpfully. "In the church, in the ground." One or two people laughed.

Mrs Buckley glared at them and they stopped.

She turned back to Tom. "*How* did you find it?" she said.

"Well," said Tom, and he launched into a whole speech about going to do the flowers with me and my mum. Everyone stared at me then, including Mrs Buckley. I felt my face go hot. But Tom was still rabbiting on and everyone turned back. He went on about the new boiler and the deep hole and the masses of bones, and only then did he get to the skull.

"It's a dream come true," he finished. "It's got to be the best in my collection."

"And you have a very good collection," acknowledged Mrs Buckley. "But..."

This is it, I thought, this is it. She's going to ask him.

"Who gave it to you?"

There, it was out.

Tom didn't turn a hair. "No one," said Tom cheerfully. "It was just lying there."

Mrs Buckley stared. "Are you telling me," she said, "are you telling me that you just *took* the skull?"

Case over. Guilty as charged.

"I..." said Tom. I thought for a moment he was going to say the workman had given it to him or, worse still, that my mum had said he could have it. Perhaps he might have done, but Mrs Buckley interrupted.

"Surely," she said, and her voice was icy. "Surely you knew you couldn't just take the skull?"

Tom swallowed. No one moved.

Mrs Buckley waited.

"I'm not sure," said Tom at last.

The whole class seemed to let out its breath.

"I think you are sure," said Mrs Buckley. "I think you know you have to take that skull back to where it belongs."

Tom said nothing.

"Don't you, Tom?"

"Well..."

"As soon as possible, Tom."

Yes, yes, I thought. Before anything else happens. Then I can get some sleep. I didn't want another of those terrible dreams. I just wanted the curse to be lifted.

"Promise me, Tom. Promise me you'll take it back," said Mrs Buckley.

I heard Tom mumble something.

"Good," said Mrs Buckley. "Good. That's that then." She turned her attention to us. "Maths. I think," she said. "You'll need Maths books, rulers, compasses..."

"But, Mrs Buckley..."

We turned. At the back of the room

Milly Bateman was waving her hand in the air like an agonized jellyfish. "I haven't had my turn – and I've brought Harold!"

Chapter 4

I thought Mrs Buckley was going to say no. I thought she was going to put Milly Bateman off until another day. But she didn't.

Milly made her way to the front of the class, carrying the biscuit tin. As she passed my desk I heard little scrabbling sounds. It's a mouse, I thought. I liked mice. I wondered if Mrs Buckley did too.

Milly stood at the front. She didn't take the lid off the biscuit tin. She began her talk.

"First of all, I just want to say that when I lift Harold out, I don't want anybody shrieking or making any sudden movements."

Mrs Buckley nodded her approval. "Animals need a calm, quiet atmosphere," she said.

Milly waited until all the shuffling of feet and shifting of bodies had ceased. Then she eased the lid off the tin and brought out – a big black rat.

There were gasps. I gasped. But no one screamed. Not then anyway.

I have to admit Milly was very good with that rat. All the time she was talking to us, she was stroking him, reassuring him. Her talk was very interesting. She told us how to choose a rat and what kind of cage it should have.

"Metal or plastic is best," she said. "You can have wood but rats are very good at gnawing. They could gnaw their way out of a wooden cage."

"Does he bite?" someone asked.

"No," said Milly. "Rats only bite if they're frightened. Any sudden movement could upset them. Then they'd bite, even claw. It's their way of protecting themselves."

"What does he eat?" someone else asked. "People?"

There was a laugh. Milly smiled and patiently explained that rats needed a balanced diet – a bit of everything: bread, bird seed, vegetables, even fruit occasionally. I was really interested. I wondered if Mum would let me have a rat.

"I wouldn't mind having a rat," I whispered to Tom. He shrugged. He was pretending not to be interested. He was still sulking about his skull.

"It's a good idea sometimes to give them a dog biscuit," said Milly. Everyone laughed. "Because they're hard," said Milly. "Rats really need to gnaw. It keeps their teeth sharp and the right length."

There were lots of questions when she'd finished. I noticed that Harold was getting a bit restless. Once or twice Milly had to move her hands quickly to stop him from escaping.

Mrs Buckley noticed too.

"Perhaps you should put Harold back in his tin now," she said. "He's been very good."

"Can he do tricks?" someone called out.

"Yes," said Milly. She looked at Mrs Buckley, who nodded.

Milly put Harold on the back of her wrist and held out her arm. Quick as a flash, he ran up her arm and on to her shoulder. There he sat while Milly stroked him and talked to him. Then he ran round the back of her neck to the other shoulder.

It was impressive. Harold was so alert, so full of fun. Milly picked up a small piece of apple. Harold took it delicately in his front paws and began to eat it.

"Can we hold him?" I asked.

There was a rush forward.

"Sit down!" yelled Mrs Buckley. She turned to Milly. But Harold was fine. He was back in Milly's hands.

"If I went round," said Milly, "they could just stroke him."

"Please," we all said. We didn't want Harold put away. We liked him.

And Mrs Buckley is not mean.

"If you sit quietly," she said. "If you sit very quietly" – we sat stiller than statues – "I'll ask Milly to bring him round." She checked to make sure everyone was absolutely still. "One stroke each," she warned.

We hardly breathed. Milly made her way

round the classroom. I definitely decided to ask my mum if I could have a rat. Everyone stroked Harold. Even those who were a bit scared had a tiny stroke. Milly had almost reached Tom and me. Maybe after school I could ask Milly where she'd bought Harold. I'd got some pocket money saved up.

Milly reached our desk. Harold lay on the flat of her hand, his eyes bright, his whiskers twitching. He seemed to be enjoying all the fuss. I couldn't wait to stroke him but Milly held him out to Tom first.

Tom didn't move. He didn't want to know. He just stared into the distance.

It was awful. It was so embarrassing. I felt really sorry for Harold. So I shot my hand across to stroke him.

But it never reached him.

Harold leapt out of Milly's hands and landed on Tom's arm. Tom jumped up. Harold flew in the air. Then somehow Tom's legs got mixed up with the chair's legs and crashed backwards onto the floor. Harold landed on top of him.

I watched horrified as Harold's teeth tore at Tom's jumper. His teeth and his claws scrabbled deeper and deeper.

Then I sprang. At the same time as I grabbed Harold, Milly went to grab him too. I let go. Milly missed. Harold leapt to the floor and hurtled across the room.

People screamed and jumped on chairs and desks. I picked Tom up. He looked really pale. The front of his jumper was in shreds.

Mrs Buckley was shouting. Milly was crying. Some people were screaming, others were yelling, "I can see him! There he is! I'll get him for you!"

"SIT DOWN!" thundered Mrs Buckley.

At that moment, the door opened and two little Infants came in with a note.

"Shut the door!" shrieked Mrs Buckley. The Infants looked bewildered. They didn't know whether to come in and shut the door or go out and shut the door. So they didn't do

either. They just stood there.

Harold chose that moment to nip out from behind the waste-paper basket and scuttle across the floor right in front of them. They screamed, leapt onto the nearest desk and clung to each other crying.

Harold changed direction, veered across the room and disappeared.

Eventually, when everyone had climbed down and sat down, and the two little Infants had been lifted down, there was quiet.

"Now," said Mrs Buckley. "Turn this way and listen."

We listened.

We heard scrabbling noises at the back of the room where the box of scrap materials was stored, and all the paint and paint palettes.

"I said turn this way and *listen*!" said Mrs Buckley. We turned.

"Cheryl," she said. "You're sensible. Go and see if the hall is empty."

We waited.

Cheryl came back. She reported that the hall was empty.

"Now," said Mrs Buckley. "I am going to take everyone *with their reading book* into the hall, except you, Milly, and ... Cheryl."

Cheryl looked worried sick.

"When you have found *and caught* your rat and he is safely back *in his tin*, come and tell me. Is that clear?"

Milly nodded. Cheryl just stared. She'd gone green.

Mrs Buckley turned to us. "Is that clear?" she said.

We murmured agreement. One by one, we squeezed through the barely open door. The two Infants fled down the corridor still clutching their note. Somehow I didn't think they'd offer to deliver a message again.

"You could have been bitten to death," I whispered to Tom, once we were settled in the hall. He hadn't said a word. Not a thank you for rescuing him or anything. I noticed he seemed to be reading but he hadn't turned the page.

"It's the curse!" I persisted. "Can't you see?"

Chapter 5

At playtime we played football. That term we had proper teams and proper matches with referees and a league table – our version of the World Cup. There was even a silver cup for the winning team.

Tom was our captain. We'd all chosen him. He was the best striker in the school. But that playtime, our last practice before the Final, he was hopeless. He missed passes, shot wide, lost tackles, even tripped over the ball. His mind just wasn't on the game and I knew where it was. On the skull – on the curse. He still looked pale as a ghost.

We'd never win the Final if Tom played like that. Still, I reasoned, he had promised to take the skull back.

By tomorrow, the curse would be lifted and he'd be his usual brilliant self.

The next morning, the day of the Final, when Tom didn't call for me, I wasn't worried. Sometimes he did call for someone else. I waited as long as I could but then Mum started looking at the clock and making pointed remarks about being late. And I hated being late so I went.

"Good luck!" she called after me. "I'll have your tea ready."

I'd hardly eaten any breakfast. I was too excited.

But when Tom hadn't appeared by the time the bell rang, my excitement died. Where was he? He couldn't be late on Cup Final Day. As Mrs Buckley did the register, the whole class buzzed with the news of his absence. I began to feel sick. Perhaps he hadn't taken the skull back last night? The curse was still working, making everything go wrong!

Mrs Buckley told me to go and get changed.

"But Tom isn't here yet," I said.

She was kind. "I know," she said. "I'm sure they'll let someone else play instead."

Of course we had a substitute but...

"Can't we wait?" I asked Mr Taylor, our

games teacher. "I'm sure Tom'll be here any minute."

Mr Taylor was kind too but he wouldn't hear of postponing the game. The whole school was already on its way out to the field.

"I'm sorry, Jack," he said. "If Tom comes before we start, he can play. Otherwise, you'll have to play your substitute."

It was the longest match I've ever known. We all did our best. But with no Tom, we didn't stand a chance.

The final score was 3–0. To them.

Mr Taylor said we'd done really well. Letting three in, I thought, how does he work that out? But I knew he was only trying to be nice.

"It was bound to be difficult, not having Tom," he said. "Where is he?"

No one knew. I asked Mrs Buckley if she'd had a message but she hadn't. She thought I'd be the person to know where Tom was if anyone did. All I knew was that Tom must still have the skull.

At home time, I ran all the way to Tom's house. I went straight round to the garage. I opened the side door and looked in, and the first thing I saw was – Tom! He had his back to me, but instantly he swung round and tried to hide something behind him.

"Oh, it's you," he said, bringing out the human skull.

"I knew it!" I cried. "I knew you hadn't taken it back. No wonder everything's going wrong. And why weren't you at school today? We played the Final! We lost!"

"Well, don't blame me," said Tom.

I stared at him. "You knew we didn't stand a chance without you!" I shouted. "Where were you?"

Tom shrugged his shoulders.

"I couldn't come," he said.

"Couldn't come?" I shouted. "Oh, you had something more important to do I suppose. It was only the Cup Final. That's all."

"It wasn't like that."

"Tell me about it!" I yelled.

"If you must know!" he yelled back. "I was out looking for Sooty."

I couldn't take it in. "What do you mean you were out looking for Sooty?" I said. "Why?"

Tom turned away but I grabbed his shoulder. "Why?"

"Because she's disappeared," he said. "That's why."

"It's the skull," I said in a horrified whisper. "The curse. I warned you."

"That's stupid. It's nothing to do with the skull," said Tom. "I'm going to put a notice in the library in case anyone's seen her."

"When did she disappear?" I asked.

Tom hesitated.

"When?" I persisted.

"She didn't come home Saturday night..."

"There you are!" I said. "It *is* the skull. You know it is. You have to take it back."

Tom didn't answer. He just held the skull in his hands. Then he said, "I can't."

"But why? I'll go with you if you like. We'll go now."

Tom just looked at me. "I can't take it back," he said, "because I know I'll never get the chance to own another one."

"So you don't care about the curse?" I said. "You don't care about Sooty?"

Tom took hold of me then and yelled in my face. "Of course I care! I've been all over, trying to find her!"

"But if you take the skull back," I urged him, "Sooty will come back. The curse will be lifted."

It was so simple. I couldn't understand why he couldn't see it.

Tom pushed me away.

I watched him put the skull in his sports bag and shove it under the bench.

"Keeping it hidden, are you?" I taunted him. "Daren't put it on show? In case your dad sees it?"

"Oh, get lost!" shouted Tom.

I shrugged and left him to it.

Why should I care? If Tom wanted to keep the stupid skull, that was up to him. But I didn't want to be friends with him any more. As far as I was concerned, if I never saw him again, it was too soon. Why should I care what the curse brought down on him next?

The following day, Tom was back at school but we didn't speak.

At home time, I hung about the cloakroom until I was sure he'd had plenty of time to get well ahead of me.

As I walked up our road, I glanced across at his house. Unusually, there were lights on everywhere. Not just downstairs, upstairs as well. But I couldn't be bothered to be interested or alarmed.

From my bedroom, I looked across again. All the lights were still blazing.

I allowed myself to wonder, then, if Tom was all right. Perhaps I should just go over and see if he was.

But at that moment, the phone rang.

I heard Mum go to answer it.

"It's for you!" she called. "It's Gran."

I went downstairs.

Gran wanted to know all about the match. She's a good listener. She didn't say anything until I'd finished.

"Was Tom ill?" she asked.

I told her about Sooty's disappearance, that Tom had been out looking for her.

"Oh dear," she said. "He must have felt dreadful letting you down. But I can understand it."

Suddenly I wanted to tell Gran the whole lot, the skull, the curse... She'd sort everything out. But she lived so far away.

"It's a good job he's got a friend like you," said Gran. "You know who your friends are when you're in trouble."

I put the phone down. I should have gone over to Tom's. I saw that now. Just to make sure he was all right. Anything could have happened.

I went into the kitchen.

Dad came in.

"There's an ambulance across the road," he said. "What's happened? Do you know?"

Chapter 6

I felt ill. I felt sick.

"Oh, dear," said Mum. "I wonder if there's anything we can do." She hurried out.

"You all right?" asked Dad. "Had a bad day?"

I nodded and then shook my head. I wasn't really listening. I was thinking, It's the curse – Tom's fallen ill – they're rushing him into hospital!

Mum came back. "You should have told me sooner," she said to Dad. "By the time I got there, the ambulance was turning the corner at the end of the street."

She began to dish up the meal.

I found my voice.

"Did you see inside the ambulance?" I asked.

"Of course not," said Mum. "I told you. It was disappearing..."

"But did anyone else see?" I persisted. Surely someone had been out there watching.

"No," said Mum.

She put the plates on the table.

"I know one thing," she said as we sat down. "There's no lights on across the road..."

I dashed out of the kitchen up to my room. It was true. Tom's house was in darkness.

"You all right, Jack?" Mum called from the bottom of the stairs.

I sidled along the landing to the bathroom and flushed the toilet.

"Yes!" I called. "Won't be a minute."

I stared into the lavatory bowl, watching the water swirl round and round until there was only the foamy part lying at the bottom of the pan. I should have done something. Gran was right. I should have tried to help him.

I listened to the cistern going through the ritual of filling up. I'd told Tom to take the skull back but telling him hadn't been enough.

The cistern gurgled to its finish and was quiet. There was a knock at the bathroom door. "Are you sure you're all right?" called

Mum. "Your meal's getting cold."

I flushed the toilet again. Water poured round the side of the bowl.

"Just coming!" I called.

I put the plug in the wash-basin and ran some water, hot, then cold. I picked up the soap and washed my hands, slowly, carefully. If only I could think of something. I rubbed my hands together until the soap disappeared, and rinsed them. I'd have to go down soon. I let the water out of the basin.

And then it hit me. It was so simple.

The skull brought down a curse on anyone who removed it from its resting place. If Tom had taken the skull back to the church, the curse would have been lifted. But he hadn't – and now he was in hospital, he couldn't.

But I could.

I practically danced down the stairs.

"Well, you seem to be all right," said Mum as I wolfed down a generous portion of steak and kidney pie. "I thought perhaps you weren't feeling well."

"I'm fine now," I said.

I needed to think. I had to get the skull back to the church fast. But I couldn't just walk out. There'd be questions.

Dad probably wouldn't notice. He'd already finished his meal and was in the sitting-room, slumped in front of the telly.

But Mum was a different matter. She'd got eyes in the back of her head.

I only needed a little while. I had to get across the road to Tom's to fetch the skull and then it would be easy. Straight down our back garden, across the lane at the bottom, and into the church. It wouldn't take more than, say, ten minutes at the most.

Just as I was wondering how I'd ever get out without Mum noticing, the phone rang. Mum went to answer it. It was her best friend! When Mum and Ella get talking, the house could take off and sail to the moon and Mum wouldn't notice!

As soon as I was outside and crossing the road, I realized I should have brought a torch. There was only just enough light from a streetlamp to see my way down the path to the side door of Tom's garage. But once inside, I switched on the light. There were the rows of skulls and skeletons and there, underneath the bench, was Tom's sports bag. I pulled it out, feeling the bulge of the skull inside. Then I switched off the light and was back across to our house in minutes.

It was really dark down our garden path, but I knew every bump and stone so I wasn't bothered. I didn't like crossing the lane though and when I opened the churchyard gate, it creaked and then swung to behind me with a clang, making me jump. The tall fir trees which bordered the churchyard stirred uneasily as I made my way slowly forward, over the uneven paving-stones.

Then the moon broke free of the clouds. Ahead of me, the tower looked terrifying, rising up into the sky like the battlements of a castle. The moon lit the path but I hated the way it also lit the gravestones looming up out of the darkness on each side. By the time I reached the door, my heart was pounding.

I took hold of the handle, turned it and made myself step inside.

The damp and cold hit me. And the stillness. It was so quiet. Only the clock's slow beat – slower than my heart's thumping – broke the silence.

I stood just inside the door. My legs had turned to jelly. I made myself move forward.

Moonlight filtered through the windows, casting eerie shadows. Statues seemed to watch me as I passed. I daren't look behind.

At last I reached the hole. I knelt down, unzipped the bag, reached inside and brought out – Tom's football.

My mind went blank. Wildly, I scrabbled round the inside of the bag. There was nothing else there. I couldn't think what to do. I stared into the bag, then a slight noise on the other side of the hole made me look up.

On the floor, as though it had never been

away, was the skull – and behind it, white in the darkness, was another face, Tom's. Pale as a ghost.

A dreadful shivering took hold of me. I was too late. The curse had killed him and his ghost had brought the skull back.

I couldn't scream and I couldn't move away. I just knelt there and shook.

The ghost spoke.

"What are you doing here?"

I tried to answer. I tried to stand up.

"The same as you," I managed to stammer.

The ghost laughed. It sounded horrible.

"But you've only brought my football!" it guffawed.

I was still shaking and I'd no intention of upsetting a ghost but there are limits. I stood up.

"Well, I didn't know that," I said. "I thought I was helping. I didn't know the curse was going to kill you and you were going to bring the skull back yourself."

"I'm not a ghost!" the ghost shrieked.

"I'm Tom. It's me!"

And whether the moonlight glimmered more brightly at that point or whether the light dawned in my brain, I don't know. But what I did know was that it was indeed Tom, not the ghost of Tom, facing me across the hole.

"What are you doing here?" I shouted.

"No, I said that!" grinned Tom.

"You're supposed to be at the hospital," I shrieked. "You went in the ambulance."

"No, I didn't," said Tom. "Mum did. The baby came early." I couldn't take it in.

"But the skull...?" I said.

"I brought it back," said Tom. "When the ambulance came. Dad said I should go round to your house but I came here instead."

He flashed a torch full in my face. "Good fun in the dark though!" He started to laugh again. "And you thought I was a ghost! You were really scared. You should have seen your face!"

Something clicked in my brain. While I'd

been worrying, fretting about him being rushed into hospital, being seriously ill; while I'd been trying to think, working out how to help, he'd been swanning back to the church with the skull tucked underneath his arm.

I wanted to hit him. I wanted to punch him right in the middle of his silly grinning face. I stepped forward...

As I fell, I saw his grin disappear. I saw it change into shocked amazement – and then I was at the bottom of the hole, looking up at the skull and Tom's white face staring down at me.

Chapter 7

Most of the story came out on the way to the hospital. Yes, I know. After all that, I was the one who ended up in hospital ... and I didn't get to go in an ambulance either, just in our car with Mum and Dad.

My right arm was really painful. As I'd fallen into the hole, I must have hit one of the pipes. Tom tried to pull me out but it was hopeless. In the end, he had to go and fetch my parents.

He was ages – and I can tell you, sitting at the bottom of that hole, in the dark, with the moon shining down on the masses of bones above me, is not an experience I ever want to repeat.

There was plenty of time at the hospital while we were waiting for my arm to be looked at, to start telling Mum and Dad what had been going on. It took my mind off the pain anyway and afterwards, at home, I finished the story. I didn't leave anything out. It was a relief in a way. Amazingly, they weren't too angry. Perhaps they thought having an arm broken in two places was enough for the time being.

Mum had a few things to say about me being out in the dark on my own, and quite a lot of things to say about Tom's part in the affair. But she let Tom in the next day when he came to see me, and wanted to know all about his new baby sister. I wanted to know about Sooty – Tom was carrying her.

"Milly Bateman had taken her in!" said Tom. "Sooty was in their garden and Milly assumed she must be a stray. She can't resist animals. But at least she brought her straight back when she saw the notice in the library."

"So Sooty didn't exactly disappear," I said.

Come to think of it, nothing had turned out as bad as it had seemed at the time.

And I remembered the workman and the way he'd winked at me. The curse of the skull had been nothing but one great, big enormous joke!

Tom's just been round, waving an article at

me from the local paper. It's about the excavations at the cathedral in town. Underneath the new visitor centre they're building, they've found all sorts of treasures.

"Including human remains," said Tom. "*Skulls!* And next Saturday it's open to the public."

He wants me to go with him. He must think I'm stupid.

"I only want to look," he says.

Now where have I heard that before?

MORE WALKER PAPERBACKS
For You to Enjoy